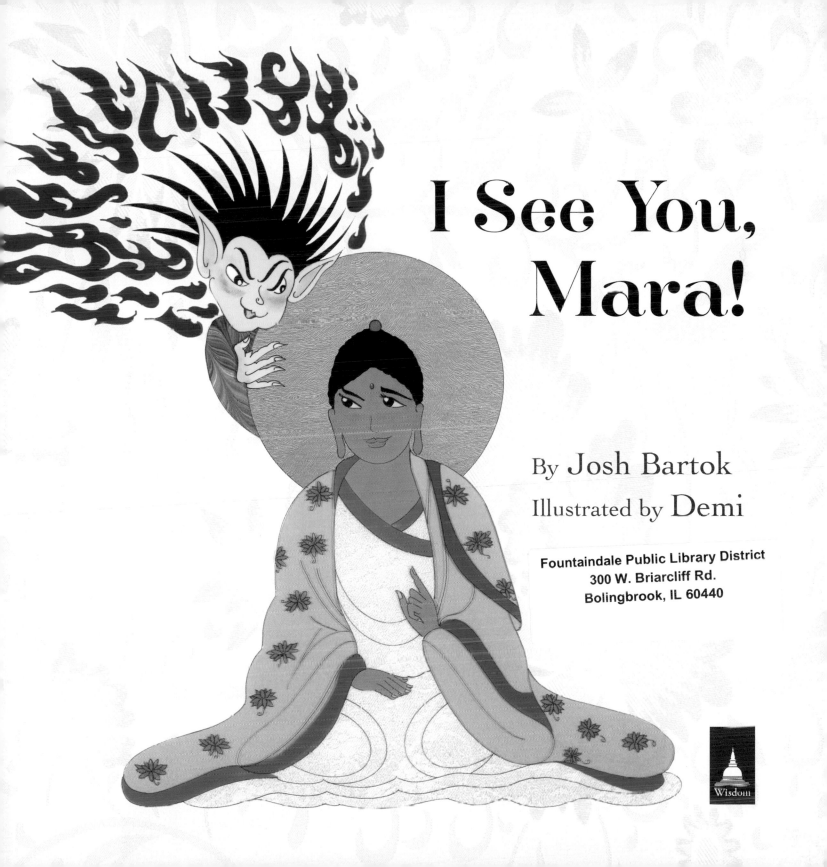

I See You, Mara!

By **Josh Bartok**

Illustrated by **Demi**

Wisdom

Dedicated to anyone who hears Mara's voice.

Wisdom Publications
199 Elm Street
Somerville, MA 02144 USA
wisdomexperience.org

Library of Congress Cataloging-in-Publication Data
Names: Bartok, Josh, author. | Demi, illustrator.
Title: I see you, Mara! / by Josh Bartok; illustrated by Demi.
Description: First. | Somerville: Wisdom Publications, 2021.
Identifiers: LCCN 2021006493 (print) |
    LCCN 2021006494 (ebook) | ISBN 9781614296850
    (hardcover) | ISBN 9781614296843 (ebook)
Subjects: LCSH: Māra (Buddhist demon)—Juvenile
    literature. | Tipiṭaka. Suttapiṭaka. Saṃyuttanikāya. |
    Buddhist demonology.
Classification: LCC BQ1332.E5 B37 2021 (print) |
    LCC BQ1332.E5 (ebook) | DDC 294.3/33—dc23
LC record available at https://lccn.loc.gov/2021006493
LC ebook record available at https://lccn.loc.gov/2021006494

ISBN 978-1-61429-685-0 ebook ISBN 978-1-61429-684-3

25 24 23 22 21
5 4 3 2 1

Cover and interior design by Gopa & Ted 2, Inc.

Printed on acid-free paper that meets the guidelines for
permanence and durability of the Production Guidelines for
Book Longevity of the Council on Library Resources.

Printed in Malaysia.

Once there was a person
(just like you, just like me),
a good-hearted person
who sat down by a tree.

This person was wise,
and the wise find what's true.

The Wise One is Buddha,
and the Wise One is you.

But there's also another;
there's one who you'll hear.

This other's called Mara,
and Mara's so often near.

Mara, he sneaks,

and Mara, she hides.

Mara plays many mean tricks—

and Mara tells lies.

Mara whispers to Buddha:
"You are weak.
  You're no good."

Mara sneaks up to Buddha:
"You can't do what you should!"

"I see you, Mara!"
the Wise One can say.

"I know you, Mara!"

then ⎯POOF!⎯ Mara's away.

But Mara comes back,
and now Mara tries **fear.**

Mara's got many **mean tricks,**
and brings all of them here.

Mara comes as
a snake,

Or a
monster with claws.

But each time Mara comes,
the Wise One can pause.

Pausing often is such a good thing to do.

Pausing will help us to find what is true.

"I see you, Mara!"
the Wise One can say.
"I know you, Mara!"

then ⎯POOF!⎯ Mara's away.

But Mara comes back,
and now Mara tries hooks.

Yet no **things** Mara offers are worth second looks.

"I see you, Mara!"
the Wise One can say.

"I know you, Mara!"

then

—POOF!—

Mara's away.

Do **you** also hear Mara?

How about **today**?

Now when **you** see Mara,

what can **you** say?

Then

POOF!

Mara's
away.

About

Mara is a character from the Buddhist tradition who is the personification of the habits of mind that cause suffering—and stories about Mara appear in the Samyutta Nikaya (specifically, the Marasamyutta), one of the oldest canonical texts of Buddhism. Known also as the Tempter, the Deceiver, or even the Killer, Mara continually tries to turn people away from the path to liberation and encourages them to remain trapped by their suffering—eliciting the energies of craving, fear, and delusion. For Buddha to triumph over Mara, they need only recognize Mara as Mara: "I see you, Mara!"—a phrase that comes directly from the ancient texts. Once Buddha says this, Mara will disappear, "sad and disappointed"—as the suttas say repeatedly. Cognates of the name Mara persist in the English language in the words *nightmare* and *murder*.

Josh Bartok is an ordained Zen priest, pastoral therapist, and editor of Dharma books with over twenty years of experience at Wisdom Publications and hundreds of books to his credit. He has degrees in cognitive science from Vassar College and in mental health counseling from the University of Massachusetts–Boston. He's the author of the popular *Daily Wisdom* series, which includes *Daily Wisdom*, *More Daily Wisdom*, *Nightly Wisdom*, and *Daily Doses of Wisdom*, and he is the coauthor (with Ezra Bayda) of *Saying Yes to Life (Even the Hard Parts)*. Additionally, he's an abstract expressionist photographer and the founding spiritual director of the Greater Boston Zen Center in Cambridge, Mass. He and Demi also collaborated on *I See You, Buddha!*

Demi was born in Cambridge, Massachusetts, into a family of renowned artists, with painting in her blood. She studied at the Instituto Allende in Guanajuato, Mexico; with Sister Corita at Immaculate Heart College in Hollywood, California; at the M.S. University in Baroda, India, while on a Fulbright Scholarship; and at the China Institute for Arts in New York City. Demi is the award-winning author and illustrator of more than three hundred bestselling children's books, including picture-book biographies of spiritual leaders such as Buddha, the Dalai Lama, Lao Tzu, Confucius, Gandhi, Jesus, Mother Teresa, Muhammad, Guru Nanak, and Hiawatha. Her titles have sold over two million copies. Numerous folktales such as *The Empty Pot* and *Liang and the Magic Paintbrush* transmit the wonder and magic of China. Her work has received many awards and accolades, among them the Christopher Award, which recognizes individuals whose work makes a positive difference in the world, and the Middle East Book Award. Her titles have also been designated American Library Association Notable Children's Books, *New York Times* Best Illustrated Books, Notable Books for a Global Society, and American Bookseller Pick of the List Books.